The Gods and Goddesses of Olympus

WRITTEN AND ILLUSTRATED BY *Aliki*

HarperCollins*Publishers*

Ancient Greece

Macedonia

Thrace

MT. OLYMPUS

Thessaly

Asia Minor

Ionian Sea

LEMNOS
HEPHAESTUS
fell here

Aegean Sea

Mysia

DELOS
APOLLO
born here

ATHENS

AEGAE
POSEIDON'S
palace

Peloponnesus

SAMOS
ZEUS & HERA
married
here

THEBES
DIONYSUS
born here

MT. CELENE
MAIA born here
HERMES born here

ORTYGIA
ARTEMIS
born here

CYTHERA
APHRODITE
born here

TRENURUM
Entrance
to Hades

Sicily

MT. IDA
ZEUS hidden here

Crete

HENNA
PERSEPHONE
abducted here

The illustrations in this book have been adapted from Greek vase paintings and sculpture,
with all due respect. The artwork was first drawn in pencil on heavy cold-press paper.
The drawings were then inked and colored with washes of gouache paints and colored pencils.

The Gods and Goddesses of Olympus.   Copyright © 1994 by Aliki Brandenberg.   Manufactured in China. All rights reserved.

Library of Congress Cataloging-in-Publication Data   Aliki.   The gods and goddesses of Olympus / by Aliki.
p.   cm.   ISBN 0-06-023530-6. — ISBN 0-06-023531-4 (lib. bdg.) — ISBN 0-06-446189-0 (pbk.)   1. Gods, Greek—Juvenile literature.
2. Goddesses, Greek—Juvenile literature.   3. Mythology, Greek—Juvenile literature.   [1. Mythology, Greek.]   I. Title.
BL782.A45   1994   93-17834   292.2'11—dc20   CIP   AC

for
Peter James Marshall

and his papou
Peter James Liacouras
with whom I first learned about
gods, goddesses, and baseball

Long, long ago in ancient Greece,

some people began telling stories to explain the mysteries of life.
Over much time, the stories—or myths—grew rich and imaginative.
The storytellers wove in their customs, beliefs, and theories about life,
death, and the wonders of nature. The myths were about gods and goddesses,
fearful monsters, brave heroes, and mysterious beauties.

People believed the myths were true. They worshiped the gods—
who they believed helped and guided them—and built temples to honor them.

According to the mythology the gods and goddesses looked and acted human.
They married each other. They laughed, loved, quarreled, and fought
with each other. But they were immortal. They lived forever
because a fluid called ichor—not blood—flowed through their veins.

The mightiest of the gods and goddesses lived in a golden palace
on Olympus—a mountain so high, the top was hidden by clouds.
They feasted on ambrosia and nectar—the food and drink of the gods.
And whenever they wished, they could change shape
and speed down to earth, to mingle with the mortals.

The awesome Olympians earned their thrones on Olympus.
They fought a fierce battle—and won.

This is the story of how it happened.
It starts at the beginning of time.

In the beginning . . .

Gaea, the Earth, grew out of a dark space named Chaos.

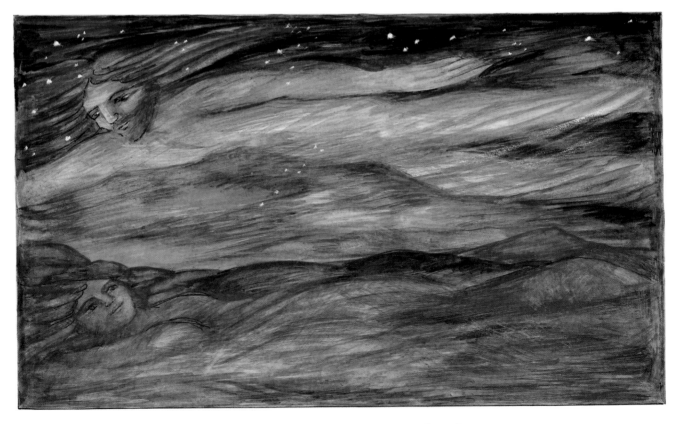

Gaea gave birth to Uranus, the sky.

Uranus rained down on young Gaea, and plants, animals, and rivers appeared.
Gaea became Mother Earth, mother of all living things—and mother of the
first gods.

Gaea and Uranus had many children.
Their firstborn were the twelve giant Titans, six girls and six boys.

ARGES, BRONTES, STEROPES

BRIAREUS, GYES, COTTUS

Later, more children were born.
Three were the mighty Cyclopes—
strong, one-eyed giants.

Three were the Hecatoncheires—
monsters each with a hundred arms
and fifty heads.

Uranus hated the Cyclopes and the Hecatoncheires, because they were ugly.
He threw them into Tartarus—the deepest pit in the Underworld.

Gaea was furious. She urged the Titans to overthrow their father
and rescue their brothers.
Only the youngest, Cronus, was brave enough.

He attacked Uranus with a sickle and banished him from the Earth.
Cronus replaced his father as Lord of the Universe.
But he was cruel and did not free his brothers from Tartarus.

Cronus married his sister Rhea, and they had many children.
But Cronus was afraid that one of them might overthrow him
just as he had overthrown his father.

So as each child was born, he swallowed it.

Rhea was horrified. When the youngest was born, she tricked Cronus. She hid the baby Zeus in a distant cave, so Cronus would not find him.

Rhea then gave Cronus a stone wrapped in a blanket.
He swallowed that instead—blanket and all.

Hidden away, Zeus was raised by gentle woodland nymphs and a nymph-goat named Amaltheia, who fed him honeyed milk. When the baby cried, the Curetes—Zeus's guards—clashed their weapons to hide the sound.

Zeus grew into the strongest of all the gods and married Metis, a Titan's daughter.

As thanks, Zeus gave the nymphs Amaltheia's horn. He made it into the cornucopia—the horn of plenty—which never emptied of food. And he put Amaltheia's image among the stars, as Capricorn.

Rhea was still angry with her husband and wanted Zeus to depose him.
But Metis, the Goddess of Prudence, was wise. She said Zeus needed help,
for Cronus had the Titans on his side.

Rhea found a way. With her help, Metis gave Cronus a drink
she promised would make him undefeatable.

Instead, it made Cronus throw up the stone and his unharmed children—
Hestia, Demeter, Hera, Hades, and Poseidon.
They were reunited, and gratefully they joined their brother.
Zeus freed their uncles from Tartarus, and together they prepared
to fight the Titans.

The Cyclopes, who were great builders and smiths, made the weapons.

They armed Zeus with a thunderbolt
that shook the universe.

They made Poseidon a trident
that could split the seas.

They gave Hades a helmet of darkness that made him invisible to his enemies.

For ten years war raged between the old gods and the new gods.
At last Cronus and the Titans were defeated and thrown into Tartarus,
to be guarded forever by their hundred-armed brothers.

Mother Earth was finally at peace.
Rule of the universe was divided among the three brothers.
Zeus was declared King of the Gods, and God of Heaven and Earth.
Poseidon became God of the Sea, and Hades God of the Underworld.

Iris, the Messenger of the Gods, had her own rainbow path to earth.

The Cyclopes built the victors a palace on Mt. Olympus, with twelve
golden thrones inside. For Zeus shared his powers with his brothers,
his sisters, six of his children, and Aphrodite, the Goddess of Love.
There the great Olympians lived forever.

ZEUS
King of the Gods
God of Heaven and Earth
Son of Cronus and Rhea

Zeus was everywhere—seen and unseen.

He changed his shape as easily as he changed the weather.
He moved the sun and the moon and put constellations in the sky.
He protected everyone—gods and mortals alike.

In anger Zeus hurled his thunderbolt to punish those who deserved it.
But he was also wise and fair, and generous with his praise.

Zeus first married Metis, but he made Hera his queen.
Zeus and Hera bickered constantly, for Zeus had many other wives—
goddesses, nymphs, and mortals—and had many children, too.

Hera was jealous of them all.

HERA
Goddess of Marriage and Childbirth
Daughter of Cronus and Rhea

Hera was beautiful and headstrong.

Zeus won her when he turned himself into a cuckoo and he flew into her arms, sheltered from the rain. Their wedding was so happy, it lasted three hundred years.

But things changed. Though Hera helped and advised Zeus and bore him children, jealousy darkened her days. She hated her husband's adventures. She schemed against his many wives and children and caused them to hide in fear.

Once, in anger, Hera even dared to steal Zeus's thunderbolt. But his temper was stronger. He hung her up from the sky with anvils tied to her feet, and freed her only when she repented.

HEPHAESTUS
God of Fire and Blacksmiths
Son of Zeus and Hera

Hephaestus was born with bad luck. He was so weak and lame,

Hera took one look at him and dropped him out of Olympus.
He fell for a day and was rescued by the sea goddess Thetis and her sisters.
They took him to their underwater grotto, and there he lived in secret.

Hephaestus's body grew strong, though he could never walk.
He became a master craftsman and made beautiful objects of gold in his smithy.
Many he gave to the goddesses as thanks for their kindness.

Nine years later Hera saw Thetis wearing an exquisite brooch
and demanded to know who had made it. When Hera heard it was Hephaestus,
she regretted her actions. She called him back to Olympus, allowed him
to marry Aphrodite, and created an even bigger workshop for him.

Hephaestus became the worker of the gods. He made them golden palaces,
chariots, weapons, and tools. For himself he invented two golden maidens
who helped him move about. His artistry was the pride of Olympus.

Aphrodite had no parents. She rose out of the sea

on a cushion of foam. She was so beautiful, love bloomed around her—
and sometimes jealousy.

Despite Hera's protests Zeus gave Aphrodite a throne on Olympus
and made her Hephaestus's wife. But she wasn't always true to her
homely husband, for Aphrodite wore a magic girdle that made love
flare up among the gods. Even Ares was a victim of her beauty,
though he loved war more.

Eros was wild and mischievous. Some say he was born at the beginning of time. Some say he was the son of Aphrodite and Ares.

Eros's greatest delight was to zip around shooting arrows of desire into innocent victims. Instantly they fell in love, whether they wanted to or not. And no one could stop him, not even Zeus.

Ares was a god not even a mother could like.

He was a cruel, bad-tempered coward who loved war.
The bloodier the battle, the better. In defeat he was a bad loser.
If he was wounded, he startled even the gods with his pitiful tears.
Ares stirred up trouble wherever he went. Except for Aphrodite,
no one wanted him around.

27

POSEIDON
God of the Sea and Earthquakes
Son of Cronus and Rhea

Poseidon was moody.

His temper could be as violent as the seas he ruled. He shook his trident, and leaping waves flooded the land. He struck the earth, and mountains erupted. When he was calm, rivers dried and islands formed.

Poseidon created the first horse, from a rock, with one blow. He raced the waves and traveled to Olympus in his golden horse-drawn chariot. Most of the time Poseidon lived in a golden underwater palace with his queen, Amphitrite, a lovely sea goddess. They had three children together, though Poseidon had many more. Like Zeus, he could not resist goddesses, nymphs, or mortals.

ATHENA
Goddess of Wisdom, War, and Arts and Crafts
Daughter of Zeus and Metis

Athena had a most unusual birth. Zeus had been warned

that if Metis bore a son, he would depose Zeus just as Zeus and Cronus
had deposed their own fathers. Though Zeus needed wise Metis's advice,
he took no chances. One day he lured Metis close with his sweet words—
and swallowed her.

Soon after, Zeus was hit by a horrible headache. He howled for help.
Hephaestus fetched his ax and split open Zeus's head. Out sprang Athena,
armed for action. Immediately she became her father's favorite advisor.

Athena was a warrior who hated war. She admired courage and
fairness and sought peaceful ways to settle fights. She also invented
many things—the flute, the trumpet, farm tools, and the olive tree.
She taught the arts of cooking, spinning, and weaving.
Athena had no time for marriage.

HERMES
Messenger of Zeus
Herald of the Gods
Son of Zeus and the nymph Maia

Hermes was born ready for action. As his mother slept in her cave,

he slipped out of his cradle and went looking for adventure.

He saw a tortoise, killed it, and invented the lyre from its shell.

As he taught himself to play the instrument, he spied his brother Apollo's cows—
and stole them. Cunningly he swept away their hoofprints, and Apollo
couldn't find them anywhere.

When little Hermes confessed his trick, his brother was furious.
But Hermes was shrewd. He knew Apollo loved music, and offered him the lyre
for the cows. Apollo gave him the cows and more, and left happily with the lyre.

Zeus was amused by his clever son but scolded him too.
Hermes promised not to steal or lie again—not much, anyway—if Zeus gave
him a throne on Olympus. Zeus couldn't resist. Hermes could talk anyone
into anything.

Hermes grew up to be Zeus's personal messenger and helper.
He traveled as fast as the wind on winged sandals. He guided souls of the dead
to Hades and brought good luck to travelers everywhere.

Goddess of the Moon, Wildlife, Hunting, and Chastity
Daughter of Zeus and the goddess Leto
Twin sister of Apollo

Artemis was just minutes old when she helped with the birth

of her twin, Apollo. Jealous Hera had been chasing their mother, Leto,
all over the world. Artemis found her a safe place to rest, carried there by
the South Wind.

One day her proud father asked Artemis what presents she would like.
Artemis knew exactly what she wanted. She asked for a bow and arrows
like Apollo's, so they could hunt together. She asked for a band
of nymphs for companions. She asked to stay young forever and never
to have to marry. Zeus granted all her wishes—and more.

Artemis was determined and fought for what she wanted.
Her arrows stung, and she could cause suffering.
But she loved animals and children and protected them.

APOLLO

God of the Sun, Music, Poetry, Archery, Healing, and Prophecy
Son of Zeus and the goddess Leto
Twin brother of Artemis

Apollo grew up quickly, as gods do. When he was four days old, he asked Hephaestus to make him a silver bow and arrows. Then off he went, to kill the dreaded serpent Python, which Hera had sent to kill his mother.

Apollo was dangerous with his arrows. He punished the guilty— sometimes with the help of Artemis, his twin sister. They were close friends, and both were great archers.

Yet Apollo was thoughtful. He advised others that one should search to know one's self. He also believed one should not overdo anything. He said: *Pan Metron Ariston*, which means "everything in moderation."

Apollo had a tender side to him, too. He healed the sick, cared for animals, and brought delight with his music. No one played the lyre as well. And no one sang as sweetly as Apollo.

HADES
God of the Underworld
Son of Cronus and Rhea

Hades was as grim and gloomy as the Underworld, where he lived.

He was also rich, for all the treasures in the ground were his.

Hades rarely left his dark Kingdom of the Dead. When Hermes brought souls of the dead to him, he prodded the unwilling ones into the shadows. He saw that none escaped. Cerberus, his three-headed dog, stood guard at the locked gate.

But Hades grew lonely and wanted a wife. Zeus said he could have his daughter Persephone. But Zeus knew she would not want to part with her mother, Demeter, to live in Hades's gloomy kingdom. Nor would Demeter let her go. So Zeus told Hades to kidnap Persephone.

Hades rode up into the brilliant sunshine—and that is what he did.

DEMETER
Goddess of the Harvest, Grain, and Fertility
Daughter of Cronus and Rhea
Mother of Persephone

Demeter and Persephone were always together.

Gentle Demeter loved her daughter and took her wherever she went
as she tended her grain fields.

But one day their joy vanished. As Persephone was out with friends
picking flowers, she disappeared. No one saw what happened—
not even Demeter. She did not see Hades charge up in his chariot and snatch
the lovely Persephone. She did not see him take her down,
down to the dark Underworld, to make her his queen.
She did not hear her scream and cry for her mother.

Demeter searched the earth for Persephone. She grew haggard
and neglected her fields. At last she heard what had happened.
Furious, she told Zeus that until Persephone was returned, she would cause
a famine—and she did. Soon fields grew barren, crops and trees withered,
animals and people starved. Zeus saw that Demeter meant her words.
He sent Hermes to fetch Persephone from Hades.

But Persephone had been tricked into eating four pomegranate seeds—
the food of the dead. That meant she could not leave Hades forever.
For four bleak months a year—one for every seed—she had to return
to the Underworld as Hades's queen. Then spring came, the land turned green,
and flowers bloomed—for Demeter and Persephone were together again.

DIONYSUS
God of Wine and Vegetation
Son of Zeus and the mortal princess Semele

Dionysus's mother was struck dead by lightning before he was born.

It was an accident caused by jealous Hera. Zeus rescued his unborn son
and sewed him up in his own thigh, and there he stayed until he was born.

Dionysus was hidden from Hera's sight and was raised among nymphs
and wild animals. But eventually Hera found him and drove him mad.

Dionysus traveled the world over, teaching the art of wine making.
With him went a band of wild satyrs and maenads. They danced in a frenzy
and raised a rumpus wherever they went. Hera had driven them mad too.

Later Dionysus recovered and, despite Hera's protests, was welcomed
into Olympus. Kind Hestia gave up her throne for him.
She was comfortable by the hearth.

HESTIA
Goddess of the Hearth
Daughter of Cronus and Rhea

Hestia
rarely left her place by the hearth. She saw that the sacred fire of Olympus never died out. She protected every household and hearth on Earth and was honored by gods and mortals alike.

Hestia, the gentlest of the Olympians, chose not to marry. She had enough to do as the peacemaker of her quarrelsome family.

Yet despite all their quarrels, there were harmonious times, too. Times when they all—each unique god and goddess of Olympus—ascended to their thrones.

And they were magnificent.

DEMETER
with
Persephone

HERMES

HEPHAESTUS

APHRODITE
with
Eros

ARES

HERA

HADES

ZEUS

POSEIDON

ATHENA

APOLLO

ARTEMIS

DIONYSUS

HESTIA

47

In this book are just a few of the many Greek myths
that have been told over thousands of years. In various versions
the myths have been passed on to us—first orally, then written down
by scholars through the ages. The myths have influenced many cultures.
Even the Romans modeled their gods and goddesses on the Greek ones.

The myths have endured the test of time. Even today, the gods
are valued for their human qualities, their humor, their lessons,
and their wisdom. They have become part of our lives in ways
we don't even notice.

The next time you hear a clap of thunder, or feel the wind,
or see golden wheat swaying in the fields, or hear exquisite music,
what will you think? Is that Zeus shaking his thunderbolt,
or Hermes flying past? Is it Demeter playing with her Persephone?
Is that Apollo's song filling our ears?

They are still with us.